SUPERGIRL IS PATIENT

Written by
CHRISTOPHER HARBO

Illustrated by
GREGG SCHIGIEL

SUPERGIRL based on characters created
by Jerry Siegel and Joe Shuster
by special arrangement with
the Jerry Siegel family

PICTURE WINDOW BOOKS
a capstone imprint

Supergirl is patient. She doesn't mind waiting for her chance to help. People know she will never tire of keeping them safe.

When Supergirl stands in line, she calmly waits her turn.

Supergirl is patient because she never cuts ahead.

When Supergirl has a question, she politely raises her hand.

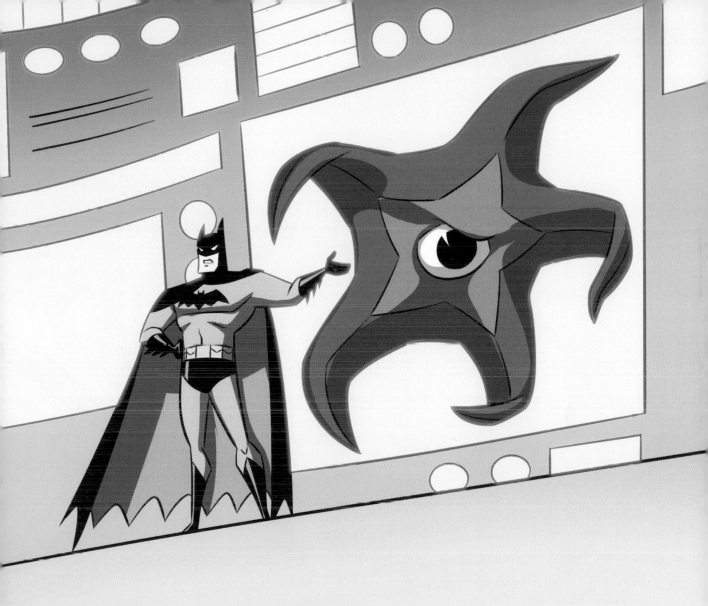

Supergirl is patient because she waits
to be called on and doesn't interrupt.

When Supergirl tackles a problem, she solves it step by step.

Supergirl is patient because she takes her time to do things well.

When Supergirl trains, she doesn't quit when she fails.

Supergirl is patient because she practices to get better.

When someone makes a mistake,
Supergirl doesn't get angry.

Supergirl is patient because she stays calm and offers to help.

When something slows her down,
Supergirl doesn't get upset.

Supergirl is patient because she waits
until she is ready to keep moving.

When people try to annoy her,
Supergirl simply ignores them.

Supergirl is patient because she doesn't
let little things bother her.

When someone is in trouble, Supergirl stops what she's doing to help.

Supergirl is patient because she always puts others before herself.

Whenever Supergirl catches crooks,
she sticks with her plan.

Supergirl knows that being patient always pays off!

SUPERGIRL SAYS...

- Being patient means waiting your turn in line, like when I wait to take a picture with Wonder Woman.

- Being patient means taking your time to do a job well, like when I disable Brainiac's ship one step at a time.

- Being patient means not getting upset when someone or something delays you, like when I stay calm until I can free myself from Killer Frost's ice block.

- Being patient means ignoring people who try to annoy you, like when I tune out the unkind words from the members of the Legion of Doom.

- Being patient means being the very best you that you can be!

GLOSSARY

annoy (uh-NOI)—to make someone lose patience or feel angry

delay (di-LAY)—to make someone or something late

disable (diss-AY-buhl)—to take away the ability to do something

ignore (ig-NOR)—to take no notice of something

interrupt (in-tuh-RUHPT)—to start talking before someone else has finished talking

practice (PRAK-tiss)—to keep working to improve a skill

READ MORE

Harbo, Christopher. *The Flash Is Caring*. DC Super Heroes Character Education. North Mankato, Minn.: Capstone Press, 2018.

Regan, Lisa. *Wait Your Turn, Tilly.* You Choose. New York: Enslow Publishing, 2018.

Shepherd, Jodie. *Kindness and Generosity: It Starts with Me.* Rookie Read About It. New York: Children's Press, 2016.

INTERNET SITES

FactHound offers a safe, fun way to find Internet sites related to this book. All of the sites on FactHound have been researched by our staff.

Here's all you do:

Visit *www.facthound.com*

Type in this code: 9781515840220

DC Super Heroes Character Education
is published by Picture Window Books
A Capstone Imprint
1710 Roe Crest Drive
North Mankato, Minnesota 56003
www.mycapstone.com

Editor: Julie Gassman
Designer: Charmaine Whitman
Art Director: Hilary Wacholz
Colorist: Rex Lokus

Cataloging-in-Publication Data is available at the
Library of Congress website.
ISBN: 978-1-5158-4022-0 (library binding)
ISBN: 978-1-5158-4286-6 (paperback)
ISBN: 978-1-5158-4026-8 (eBook PDF)

Printed and bound in the USA.
PA49